This book is a work of fiction. Any references to historical events, real people, or real places are used fictitiously. Other names, characters, places, and events are products of the author's imagination, and any resemblance to actual events or places or persons, living or dead, is entirely coincidental.

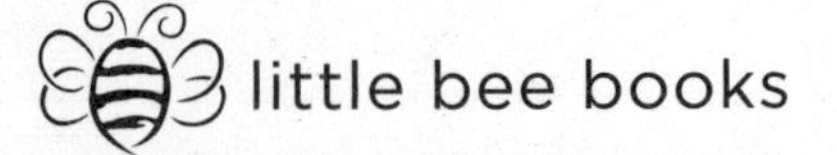

An imprint of Bonnier Publishing USA
251 Park Avenue South, New York, NY 10010

Manufactured in the United States of America LAK 1217
ISBN: 978-1-4998-0603-8 (hc)
First Edition 10 9 8 7 6 5 4 3 2 1
ISBN: 978-1-4998-0602-1 (pbk)
First Edition 10 9 8 7 6 5 4 3 2 1

Library of Congress Cataloging-in-Publication Data is available upon request.

littlebeebooks.com
bonnierpublishingusa.com

Tales of SASHA

The Royal Island

by Alexa Pearl
illustrated by Paco Sordo

little bee books

Contents

CHAPTER 1

A Wild Ride

"We found the rainbow!" cheered Sasha.

The rainbow shimmered and glowed in the pale blue sky.

"It's so close. We should fly faster to reach it sooner," said Wyatt.

Kimani laughed. "We? I think you mean Sasha and I should fly faster."

Kimani flapped her purple wings and Sasha flapped her gray wings. Wyatt couldn't flap any wings, because he didn't have any. He was an ordinary horse. He wasn't a flying horse, like Sasha and Kimani.

But Wyatt was up in the sky anyway.

The enchanted plant pixies had wrapped their strong vines around Wyatt. The vines held him in a kind of hammock. The tiny pixies grabbed on to Sasha and Kimani's manes, and the flying horses carried Wyatt through the air.

Sasha was quite proud of her horse-carrying invention.

The three horse friends were on a mission. “We must go around the rainbow to get to the Royal Island,” said Sasha.

"Full speed ahead!" cried Wyatt.

"Excuse me . . . full speed?" Kimani's violet eyes twinkled with mischief. "Did you hear him, Sasha?"

"I did." Sasha's gray eyes also twinkled.

Sasha and Kimani put on a burst of speed. A gust of wind washed over their faces. The plant pixies tightened their grip so Wyatt would stay safe in the harness.

A puffy cloud floated in. Sasha and Kimani dipped underneath it. Then they soared high over the next cloud. Under and over.

"Whoa!" Wyatt grew dizzy with all the swoops and dips. He closed his eyes. Oh, no! That made it much worse. He felt like a kite caught in a hurricane.

"Wyatt's looking a little bit green," Sasha called to Kimani.

"So? I like green horses," teased Kimani.

All flying horses had bright-colored coats. Kimani herself had a purple coat.

"I don't want to be green." Wyatt liked being an ordinary white horse. "Slow down, please!"

The rainbow arched across the sky. They flew around it, then slowed.

"Are you okay?" Sasha asked Wyatt.

Wyatt nodded.

Now they were gliding high above the sea. White-tipped waves crashed far below. Looking at them made him even queasier.

"Where's the Royal Island?" asked Sasha. Below them, the sea stretched on and on to the horizon. There was no island in sight.

Sasha had been sent by Sapphire to meet someone very special on the island. Sapphire ruled the herd of flying horses that lived in Crystal Cove.

Flying horses!

Sasha still couldn't believe it. Up until a couple of weeks ago, she hadn't known flying horses even existed. Sasha had thought she was an ordinary horse. She grazed in the fields. She went to school. Then one day, the white patch on her back began to itch—and wings popped out. Sasha could fly!

That's when the excitement began.

"How do we find the island?" Sasha looked to her right, then she looked to her left. "I don't know which way to go."

"Special delivery!" boomed a voice behind them. The toucan flew up beside them.

"Next time, ask for directions *before* you go on a long journey."

"Good point," agreed Sasha. "Can you help us?"

The toucan was Sapphire's messenger. With his colorful beak, he handed her a pair of goggles. "Put these on. The words will lead you."

"Thank you," Sasha said as Collie helped her place them on her head.

"Waste no time," warned the toucan. "The horses you are to meet will leave the Royal Island tomorrow night."

"Is it far?" asked Wyatt.

But the toucan had already flown away.

"Let's see," Sasha said, and Collie pulled the goggles over Sasha's eyes.

CHAPTER 2 Pink Cloud Magic

Sasha looked into the goggles. Tiny bits of colors danced before her eyes like in a kaleidoscope. Slowly, they came together into a message!

FLY W

Sasha blinked. "What's W?"

"That means west." Kimani pointed her hoof off in the distance. "We need to fly that way."

Sasha twisted the kaleidoscopic goggles once more. The flecks of colors swirled, but the picture didn't change. "It must give only one direction at a time. We'll fly west, and then check again."

The three horses soared through the sky.

"Do you think you're going to meet you-know-who on the island? They have to be there, right?" Wyatt asked Sasha.

"Shhh! Don't say their names!" warned Sasha. "I don't want to jinx it."

Sasha was the Lost Princess of the flying horses and the daughter of the King and the Queen. When she was a baby, they had left her with non-flying horses to keep her safe. Sasha thought about her adopted mother and father. They all loved one another, but she still wanted to meet the King and Queen.

"Watch out!" Kimani jolted Sasha out of her thoughts.

Magical butterflies swarmed around them. Their orange-and-black wings tickled the horses' noses and ears.

"Go left!" cried Kimani.

They swerved around the butterflies—and nearly bumped into five honking geese!

"Go right!" cried Kimani.

They swerved around the geese.

"Whoa!" Wyatt gulped. "What's with all the air traffic?"

Sasha looked into the goggles again. The bits of color swirled around before another message appeared: GO TO PINK.

"It must mean those pink clouds," said Kimani.

They flew toward them.

"The clouds are pink cotton candy!" Wyatt ate a sticky mouthful.

Pink confetti rained down around them. A huge fuchsia bird flew past. Its wings whirled liked a helicopter!

"Look at all this magic! We must be getting close to the Royal Island." Sasha was excited and nervous at the same time.

"The sky is changing color. Something is . . . strange." Kimani sounded worried.

The sky had turned from blue to purple to red. The breeze grew stronger. The confetti spun about. Then a fierce wind began to blow right at them. The wind made it hard for Sasha and Kimani to flap their wings.

"The butterflies and geese were flying away from this bad weather," guessed Wyatt. "Should we turn around, too?"

"We can't. I want to see you-know-who," said Sasha. "We'll be okay."

Then a strong wind made her tilt in the air. Wyatt gave a queasy cry at the sudden movement.

"Don't worry. We're holding onto you," promised Sasha.

Big, bubbly raindrops the size of small water balloons fell from the sky. The wind gusted. The raindrops burst, splashing them with fizzy water. Sasha and Kimani couldn't see where they were going.

And then—*BOOM!*

CHAPTER 3

Red Sky Storm

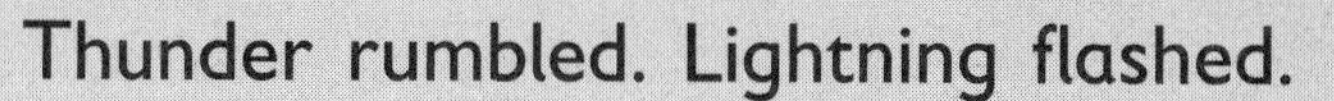

Thunder rumbled. Lightning flashed.

Sasha's ears flattened to her head. She tried not to be scared, but it wasn't easy.

Just think about flying, she told herself.

It was tricky to fly in a straight line through the wind and driving rain. Sasha and Kimani struggled to keep Wyatt steady between them as they battled the powerful storm.

"Sasha!"

Sasha heard her name above the roar of the wind. She crossed her eyes. Her plant pixie friend, Collie, sat on her snout.

A fizzy raindrop exploded in her face, and Sasha shook the water from her goggles.

Collie grabbed onto Sasha's forelock, so she wouldn't slip off. "This storm is too strong and the plant pixies are too tiny," Collie said. "We need to leave or we'll blow away in the storm. The hummingbirds have come to take us home."

Through the rain, Sasha saw the plant pixies crawl out of Kimani's mane. They climbed onto the hummingbirds' backs.

"What about Wyatt?" cried Sasha. Their vines were holding him in place. Without them, he'd fall into the sea.

"We double-knotted the vines and tied them tightly to your manes," said Collie. "He'll be safe. We promise."

Collie kissed Sasha on her nose and then climbed onto her hummingbird. All the plant pixies flew off.

Sasha looked over at Wyatt, hanging between them. He was scared, too.

Whoosh!

A huge burst of wind whirled the three of them around. Sasha wasn't sure which direction she was flying in.

Whoosh!

Another gust hit. Sasha lowered her head—and the cord holding the goggles slipped off her head.

Sasha cried out as the goggles fell down, down, down, and splashed into the sea below.

"Oh, no!" cried Sasha. "How will we find our way to the Royal Island without those goggles?"

"This storm is getting worse," Kimani said. "We have to stop flying through it." The wind whipped her braided tail.

"How can we do that?" asked Sasha.

"Is that land?" Wyatt pointed out a tiny island in the sea right below them. It had a tall mountain ringed by sand. "I vote we spend the night there." More than anything, Wyatt wanted his four hoofs back on solid ground.

Sasha and Kimani agreed.

The horses touched down on the mountain.

The rain poured, and the sky turned dark red. The friends huddled together in a shallow cave in the mountainside and quickly fell asleep.

CHAPTER 4 Hello? Anyone Here?

Sasha opened her eyes.

Where I am? she wondered.

She wasn't with her family under their cottonwood tree in Verdant Valley. She wasn't with the flying horses in the caves of Crystal Cove either.

She was on a mountain surrounded by a calm sea. The sky was a soft blue. The sun was high in the sky. Kimani and Wyatt snuggled next to her, still asleep.

Then she remembered the storm.

"Wake up." She gently shook her two friends. "The storm is over. We're on an island now."

"What island?" Kimani yawned. "Is it the Royal Island?"

Sasha shook her head. "I don't think so. There's only a mountain on this tiny island. I don't see any flying horses."

Wyatt pulled the pixies' vines off his body. Then he stood and called out, "Hello? Hello!"

Kimani joined him. "Anyone here? Hello!"

The only answer was the echo of their voices.

"Maybe whoever lives here is still asleep," said Sasha.

Kimani pointed to the sun directly overhead. "We slept for a long time. It's lunchtime now."

"That's why I'm so hungry," said Wyatt.

"You're always hungry," teased Kimani.

"Lunchtime?" cried Sasha. "You-know-who are leaving the Royal Island tonight! We're running out of time. I need to get there *now*." She got ready to fly again.

"Whoa! Keep those hooves of yours on the ground," called Wyatt.

"Why?"

"We've got three problems," said Wyatt. "One: We got blown around during the storm, so we have no idea where we are. Two: You lost the goggles, so we don't know where the Royal Island is. Three: How can I fly without the plant pixies?"

Sasha cringed. "You're right! What will we do now?"

"We should wait. The toucan or a flying horse will come rescue us," said Kimani.

"Okay, but when?" asked Sasha.

Kimani shrugged. "First, they need to figure out we're lost. After that they need to look for us. . . ."

Sasha couldn't believe it. They'd never get to the island in time!

"We shouldn't have to wait," said Wyatt. "I'm sure there's someone on this tiny island who can help us."

The three friends set off down the mountain.

CHAPTER 5

Lost and Found

A skinny path led down the mountain. Sasha walked in front. Wyatt walked in the middle. Kimani walked in back.

Wyatt stopped to munch a few yellow flowers. Kimani tumbled into him.

"Seriously? Do you really need to eat those right now?" Kimani huffed.

"I do! They taste like cheddar cheese." He licked his lips.

"Cheese flowers? How strange!" Sasha looked around. The mountain was gray rock with yellow flowers scattered about. No birds chirped. No frogs croaked. It was very quiet.

"Keep going." Kimani nudged Wyatt. "The sun is hot and I'm thirsty."

"I don't see fresh water anywhere." Sasha turned her head to look in every direction. "I don't see anything on this island. I think we should fly away now."

“If we fly in the wrong direction, we’ll get more lost than we already are,” said Kimani.

“Can we really be more lost than how lost we are now?” asked Sasha.

“Absolutely,” said Kimani. “Let’s first see what’s at the bottom of the mountain.”

They made their made their way to the rocky shore below. Tiny pebbles pressed into their hooves as they walked toward the sea.

Sasha had the strangest feeling that someone was watching them. She glanced over her shoulder. There was no one there.

"Hello? Hello!" called Wyatt again. He must have felt it, too.

The only sound was the soft lapping of the waves nearby.

"There's nothing here. I don't even see a spider or a snail or a bug," said Kimani.

"We're totally alone," agreed Wyatt.

"Not totally," whispered Sasha. "Look."

She tilted her head toward a big rock. A teapot and two teacups were perched on top of it.

“How did those get there?” whispered Wyatt.

Sasha walked over. Her friends followed. The teapot and teacups were made of delicate china. Pictures of starfish and coral were painted on them.

Sasha touched the teapot. “It’s still warm.”

She looked inside the cups. “There’s something in one.” She took a sip of pale green liquid. “It tastes like kelp tea.”

“Someone *is* on this island,” said Wyatt.

“And he or she was just here drinking this tea!” cried Sasha.

CHAPTER 6 The Trick

"Hello?" called Sasha.

She and Wyatt and Kimani searched the beach, the rocks around it, and the mountain. No one answered their calls. Nothing scurried about. No one made any noise.

The island seemed totally empty—except for the tea set.

"It's already late afternoon. You-know-who leaves the Royal Island tonight. I don't think we'll get there in time." Sasha hung her head sadly. "There's no one here to give us directions."

"Don't give up," said Wyatt. "Your lucky charm is still tied to your tail. That has to help us."

"It doesn't feel like it's helping," said Sasha.

"We didn't fall into the ocean. We didn't meet a shark. We all stayed together," pointed out Wyatt. "That's good luck, and we'll get more."

"I can't wait for luck. Where could the tea drinker have gone?" Sasha paced back and forth.

“Maybe she flew away,” said Kimani.

“Not everyone flies,” pointed out Wyatt.

“Okay. Maybe she swam away,” suggested Kimani.

“I think she saw two flying horses and got scared,” said Wyatt.

“Scared of us?” Kimani laughed.

“Sometimes it’s scary to see something you’ve never seen before,” explained Wyatt. “I was scared when I first saw flying horses.”

"Maybe the tea drinker has never seen *any* horses before," said Kimani. "Maybe she's scared of you, too."

Wyatt lowered his voice. "If I were scared, I would hide. I bet the tea drinker is hiding until we go away."

Sasha perked up. She had an idea! She motioned for her friends to follow along.

"There's no one here. We should go check the other side of the island," she called loudly.

"Yes! Let's leave here now," said Kimani even louder.

The three horses clomped away noisily.

But instead of leaving, they hid in some tall dune grass. They didn't want to be seen. They wanted the tea drinker to think they'd gone away.

They waited.

And waited.

Sasha flicked her tail. Kimani closed her eyes. Wyatt chewed on a flower.

Nothing happened.

But then they heard singing. A sweet melody floated over the *whoosh* of the nearby waves.

"Will you go to the sea with me?

Hand in hand, is how we'll be.
We'll dive for shells and bells,
and toss sand dollars in wishing wells."

"Someone is here," whispered Sasha.

The three horses hurried out from their hiding place. They couldn't believe their eyes.

A mermaid was drinking tea and singing!

CHAPTER 7

Mermaid Tea Party

"Oh!" cried the mermaid. She was as surprised to see the three friends as they were to see her.

For a moment, they all stared at one another. The mermaid had hair the color of maple sugar. Seaweed swirled through it. Dozens of shell necklaces hung around her neck. The silver scales of her fish tail shimmered in the bright sun.

"You look like a girl *and* like a fish!" cried Wyatt.

"What's so crazy about that?" The mermaid pointed to Kimani and Sasha. "They look like a horse *and* like a bird."

Sasha giggled. "You're right. We most certainly do."

The mermaid giggled, too. "We're all mash-ups."

"Not me." Wyatt suddenly felt left out.

The mermaid gave him a smile. "You'd look nice with a fin or two. Maybe I could get you some."

"If I had fins, I'd swim away," said Wyatt. "Can you help us find our way off this island?"

"Leave? Already?" The mermaid waved her arms. Her shell bracelets clicked together. "But we must have tea and cockle cakes first."

"Count me in," said Kimani. She was thirsty.

"A quick cup of tea would be nice." Sasha was in a hurry, but she didn't want to be rude.

The mermaid poured the tea. She used large conch shells for two extra cups. "My name is Avery Alexis Amelia."

Kimani introduced herself, and then Sasha and Wyatt.

"Do you know the Royal Island?" Sasha asked Avery.

Avery twirled a piece of her hair as she thought. "There are many islands in this sea."

"The island has flying horses," said Sasha. "It's magical."

"I have heard about a magical island ruled by a flying king and queen," said Avery.

"That's it!" cried Sasha. "How do we get there?"

"If you dive deep off the coast, you'll come to a coral reef. Swim around the cave where the moray eel lives. Then follow the school of clownfish. They can lead you to the island." Avery flicked her tail as she spoke. "I can swim there with you if you like."

"We're *flying* horses," said Kimani. "If not on the ground, we travel in the sky."

"Swimming is the only way I know," said Avery.

"We don't dive or swim," said Wyatt. He sighed. "I guess we're here until someone finds us."

Avery was happy that they were staying. "More tea?"

As the group sipped their kelp tea, Sasha watched the sun set. Her chance to meet the King and Queen was just about gone.

“Cheer up.” Avery gave Sasha a cockle cake. Avery’s necklaces brushed against Sasha’s cheek as she leaned over.

Sasha saw the glimmer of brass. She took a closer look. *Could it be? Was it really?*

“Avery, are those goggles around your neck?” she asked.

“Do you like them? I found them on the sea floor this morning,” said Avery.

"Those are my missing goggles!" Sasha hugged Avery. "You're amazing! You've just saved us. Now we can get to the Royal Island."

"With these shiny things?" Avery raised the cord and looked at the goggles.

"There's a magic map inside," said Sasha.

"Will the goggles still give us directions?" asked Kimani.

"Let's find out," Sasha said. Avery pulled the goggles over Sasha's eyes.

CHAPTER 8 Into the Sunset

"The goggles are working," called Sasha.

Bits of color swirled right before her eyes. A message soon appeared: INTO SUNSET.

"We need to fly into the sunset to get to the Royal Island." Sasha clicked her hind hooves together. "We can get there in time if we leave right now!"

Kimani opened her wings. "Let's go!"

"Not me," said Wyatt.

"What? Why?" Sasha whirled around.

"I can't be carried without the plant pixies and their vines, remember?" he said.

Sasha had forgotten about that. She didn't want to go without Wyatt.

"Oh! I know a way to get Wyatt there." Avery gave a loud whistle.

Suddenly an enormous blue whale rose up out of the sea.

"Oscar will give Wyatt a ride," said Avery.

"A ride?" cried Wyatt. "On a whale?"

"You'll stand on his back. It's just like surfing," said Avery. "Here, I'll help you."

"I'm not so sure—" started Sasha.

Wyatt looked at the whale. Then he looked at Sasha. He knew how important this trip was. He wouldn't make her miss it.

"I've got this, Sasha. I'll ride on the whale. You and Kimani fly ahead. I'll meet you there." Wyatt pointed to the sky. "It's almost sundown. Hurry!"

Sasha and Kimani said goodbye to Avery and soared into the sunset.

After they'd flown for a few miles, a silver horse swooped out from behind a cloud.

"Sasha! We've been waiting for you!" The silver horse pointed his wing downward. "The Royal Island is over there. Hurry! Land in that clearing."

The silver horse stayed airborne as Sasha and Kimani zoomed down. They looked around. The large island was filled with tall trees. There were horses, hedgehogs, pigs, and poodles—and they *all* had wings!

"Excuse me," Kimani said to a flying pig. "Are the King and Queen still here?"

Sasha held her breath. Was she too late?

"They're in their tree house," said the pig.

Sasha hugged the flying pig. She had made it in time!

"Which tree house is theirs?" Kimani looked up. It looked like all the animals on the island lived in the trees.

"That one." The pig pointed to the biggest tree house in the tallest tree. It glittered with silver and gold.

Sasha and Kimani flew up to it. A bronze horse stood guard at the door. He stopped Kimani. "Only the Lost Princess may enter."

"But Kimani is my friend," Sasha told the guard.

"It's okay. I'll fly back down to the beach." Kimani pointed back to the sea. A whale was swimming toward the shore—with a horse on its back. "Wyatt's surfing in now. Wow! He's really brave."

The guard opened the door to the tree house, but Sasha didn't move. What if the King and Queen didn't like her? What if she didn't like them?

"You can do this." Kimani nodded toward Sasha's good luck charm. "Luck travels with you."

Sasha smiled at her friend, then stepped inside.

CHAPTER 9 The King and Queen

Two horses stood inside the royal tree house. One had a pure white coat. The other had a midnight-black coat. Both were tall and strong. Both sparkled from head to hoof. Both looked very regal.

Sasha stood quietly and watched all the activity around them.

Hedgehogs brushed the King and Queen's manes.

Poodles packed their bags.

A pig unrolled a scroll of paper and read it to them.

The King and Queen gave orders. They solved problems. They made plans for all the flying animals.

Then they saw Sasha. They rushed over to her.

"It's you!" cried the King.

"You're so . . . beautiful!" cried the Queen.

Sasha didn't know what to say. Her eyes darted around the tree house. She spotted a long, wooden table with framed pictures on top. A photo from when she was a baby. A photo of her first steps in Verdant Valley. A photo of her playing with her sisters. A photo of her going to school with Wyatt.

The Queen saw where Sasha was looking. "We've watched you grow up. We left you in Verdant Valley to keep you safe, but you were never gone from our hearts."

"We made a good choice. Your family in Verdant Valley is kind and loving. They protected you and taught you well," said the King.

Sasha nodded. Her family in Verdant Valley was the best. Finally, she found her voice. "Why did you . . . leave me with them?"

"It wasn't an easy choice, Sasha," said the King. "The Queen and I must fly all over the world, helping all the flying animals. We're never in one place very long. It wouldn't have been a good life for a young horse to stay with us. We wanted you to have friends, siblings, and a normal life."

"There was also a lot of danger," explained the Queen. "The plant pixies were our enemies. Many others wished you harm, too. We didn't want them to find you. The best way to protect you was to hide you among the ordinary horses."

"We were always watching you," said the King. "If something went wrong or you weren't happy, we would have come for you."

"I was happy," agreed Sasha.

She looked closely at the King and Queen. She noticed her ears looked like the King's ears. Her eyes looked like the Queen's.

"Your royal highness," interrupted the pig, "you must fly off now, while the time is right."

The Queen sighed. “We have important work to do in another part of the kingdom. I wish we had more time to visit with you.”

“I can come, too,” offered Sasha.

“Not this time,” said the King. “You have more growing up and learning to do. There is still danger out there.”

"We'll come back to see you," promised the Queen. "Will you help us with something now that you have your wings and know that you are a princess?"

"Sure," said Sasha. "What do you need me to do?"

CHAPTER

10 Going Home

"We want the flying and non-flying horses to be friends," the Queen told Sasha.

Sasha pointed out the window. Kimani was helping Wyatt off the whale. "See? I've already done that."

"Yes, but we want *all* the horses in Verdant Valley and Crystal Cove to be friends. We should work together to protect one another," said the Queen. "Will you be in charge of the Summer Solstice celebration? It will be a big party to bring all horses together."

"Yes, I'll do it!" Sasha liked parties.

The King stared out the window. "Why is your friend Wyatt riding a whale? I've never seen a horse do that."

Sasha explained the trouble they'd had getting Wyatt from place to place without wings. They'd gotten very creative!

"It's important to have your friends by your side." The King gave her a huge, rolled-up leaf. "This works like a magic carpet. Wyatt can use it to fly anywhere with you."

"That's amazing!" cried Sasha.

The King and Queen kissed Sasha goodbye.

Kiamni and Wyatt found Sasha and they all watched the King and Queen fly away.

"I liked the King and Queen," said Sasha.

Wyatt grinned. "You said their names. No more jinxing?"

"Nope." Sasha thought about her visit. "I'm glad I was able to meet them. Someday I'll talk with them more, but you know what? Right now, I just want to go back home."

"Now?" Kimani was surprised. "After we flew through a storm and had tea with a mermaid to get here?"

"I even rode a whale to make this trip!" said Wyatt.

"You're the best friends," said Sasha, "but there's no reason to stay."

"Yes, there is. I can't get back to Verdant Valley. I'm not surfing on a whale or being wrapped in vines again," said Wyatt.

Sasha unrolled the magical leaf. "Hop on. From now on, you'll travel in comfort *and* style."

Wyatt tried it out. "Awesome! I can fly!"

Kimani opened her wings. "This will be fun!"

"Let's go!" Sasha had her good luck charm, her kaleidoscope goggles, and clear skies ahead.

The three friends soared together—over the clouds and around the rainbow.

Read on for a sneak peek
from the eighth book in the
Tales of Sasha series!

#8
Tales of
SASHA
Showtime!
by Alexa Pearl
illustrated by Paco Sordo

CHAPTER

1 Dance Party

"Let's dance!" called Sasha.

Sasha swished her tail. She tapped her hooves. She trotted in a circle with her sisters, Zara and Poppy.

"Make room for me," Kimani said, dancing into their circle. She high-stepped and pranced.

"Go, Kimani! Go, Kimani!" chanted Sasha. Her sisters joined in.

Kimani twirled. Her purple wings fluttered. She rose above the grass.

"Whoa! Keep those hooves on the ground," Sasha warned her friend.

"Oops! I forgot I was in Verdant Valley," said Kimani.

Kimani was a flying horse. She lived in Crystal Cove with other flying horses.

The horses in Verdant Valley didn't fly. None of them had wings, except for Sasha. She'd only just found out that she was a flying horse, too!

Twinkle danced over to the group. She raised her front legs and twirled on her hind legs. Sasha cheered. Her friend from Verdant Valley was a great dancer!

"Coming in!" Wyatt clopped into the circle. He tried to lift his hooves. "Whoops!" He knocked into Zara. "Pardon me!" He then knocked into Poppy. Wyatt backed out of the circle, his head low. "I'm too clumsy to dance."

"No, you're not." Sasha gave her best friend an encouraging nuzzle. "And even if you are, it doesn't matter. It's a welcome-home celebration for all of us."

Wyatt and Sasha had just come home

from the Royal Island. Sasha had met her birth parents, the King and Queen of the flying horses, for the first time.

Sasha waved her adoptive mother and father over to join the circle.

"I twisted my ankle in the field. I can't dance today," her mom said.

"Count me out, too," added her dad.

"Big surprise," joked Sasha. Her dad didn't dance . . . ever.

Suddenly, a glossy black bird soared down from the clouds.

The toucan had come from Crystal Cove. He was the special messenger for the flying horses. He landed gently on Kimani's back.

"Greetings! I have a message for Sasha from the King and Queen," he said. "The Summer Solstice is tomorrow."

“What’s that?” asked Wyatt.

“It’s the first day of summer and the longest day of the year,” explained Kimani. “The sun shines for the longest time tomorrow.”

“Sasha, as the Lost Princess of the flying horses, it’s time for your first assignment,” said the toucan. “You are now in charge of the Summer Solstice celebration.”

“Okay!” said Sasha. “I’ll throw together a small party for the occasion.”

“Oh, it’s not going to be small. Not at all.” The toucan shook his head.

“What do you mean?” asked Sasha.

“Per the King and Queen’s orders, all the flying horses of Crystal Cove will gather in Verdant Valley to celebrate with the non-flying horses and come together as one," explained the toucan. "This party is a *very* big deal."

All the horses gathering in Verdant Valley? Sasha had been thinking something small, not an epic celebration!

"I have a to-do list for you." The toucan said, pulling a scroll of paper from under his wing. He unrolled it . . . and unrolled it . . . and unrolled it some more. The list went on and on and on!

"Sasha is too young to throw such an important party," said her mom.

"No, I can handle this." Sasha didn't want her family to think she couldn't do it. She was the Lost Princess. A princess should be able to throw a big party. Sasha forced herself to stand taller. "I'm sure of it."